THE VALOR
of Cappen Varra

THE VALOR

of Cappen Varra

Poul Anderson

ÆGYPAN PRESS

This story was first published *Fantastic Universe*, January 1957.

Special thanks to Greg Weeks, Stephen Blundell, and the On-line Distributed Proofreading Team (which can be found at http://www.pgdp.net).

The Valor of Cappen Varra
A publication of
ÆGYPAN PRESS

www.aegypan.com

We have said that there are many and strange shadows, memories surviving from dim pasts, in this Fantastic Universe *of ours. Poul Anderson turns to a legend from the Northern countries, countries where even today the pagan past seems only like yesterday, and tells the story of Cappen Varra, who came to Norren a long, long time ago.*

*L*et little Cappen go," they shouted. "Maybe he can sing the trolls to sleep —"

The wind came from the north with sleet on its back. Raw shuddering gusts whipped the sea till the ship lurched and men felt driven spindrift stinging their faces. Beyond the rail there was winter night, a moving blackness where the waves rushed and clamored; straining into the great dark, men sensed only the bitter salt of sea-scud, the nettle of sleet and the lash of wind.

Cappen lost his footing as the ship heaved beneath him, his hands were yanked from the icy rail and he went stumbling to the deck. The bilge water was new coldness on his drenched clothes. He struggled back to his feet, leaning on a rower's bench and wishing miserably that his quaking stomach had more to lose. But he had already chucked his share of stockfish and hardtack, to the laughter of Svearek's men, when the gale started.

Numb fingers groped anxiously for the harp on his back. It still seemed intact in its leather case. He didn't care about the sodden wadmal breeks and tunic that hung around his skin. The sooner they rotted off him,

the better. The thought of the silks and linens of Croy
was a sigh in him.

Why had he come to Norren?

A gigantic form, vague in the whistling dark, loomed
beside him and gave him a steadying hand. He could
barely hear the blond giant's bull tones: "Ha, easy
there, lad. Methinks the sea horse road is too rough
for yer feet."

"Ulp," said Cappen. His slim body huddled on the
bench, too miserable to care. The sleet pattered against
his shoulders and the spray congealed in his red hair.

Torbek of Norren squinted into the night. It made
his leathery face a mesh of wrinkles. "A bitter feast
Yolner we hold," he said. "'Twas a madness of the
king's, that he would guest with his brother across the
water. Now the other ships are blown from us and the
fire is drenched out and we lie alone in the Wolf's
Throat."

Wind piped shrill in the rigging. Cappen could just
see the longboat's single mast reeling against the sky.
The ice on the shrouds made it a pale pyramid. Ice
everywhere, thick on the rails and benches, sheathing
the dragon head and the carved stern-post, the ship
rolling and staggering under the great march of waves,
men bailing and bailing in the half-frozen bilge to keep
her afloat, and too much wind for sail or oars. Yes —
a cold feast!

"But then, Svearek has been strange since the troll
took his daughter, three years ago," went on Torbek.
He shivered in a way the winter had not caused. "Never
does he smile, and his once open hand grasps tight
about the silver and his men have poor reward and no
thanks. Yes, strange —" His small frost-blue eyes shifted
to Cappen Varra, and the unspoken thought ran on
beneath them: Strange, even, that he likes you, the
wandering bard from the south. Strange, that he will

have you in his hall when you cannot sing as his men would like.

Cappen did not care to defend himself. He had drifted up toward the northern barbarians with the idea that they would well reward a minstrel who could offer them something more than their own crude chants. It had been a mistake; they didn't care for roundels or sestinas, they yawned at the thought of roses white and red under the moon of Caronne, a moon less fair than my lady's eyes. Nor did a man of Croy have the size and strength to compel their respect; Cappen's light blade flickered swiftly enough so that no one cared to fight him, but he lacked the power of sheer bulk. Svearek alone had enjoyed hearing him sing, but he was niggardly and his brawling thorp was an endless boredom to a man used to the courts of southern princes.

If he had but had the manhood to leave — But he had delayed, because of a lusty peasant wench and a hope that Svearek's coffers would open wider; and now he was dragged along over the Wolf's Throat to a midwinter feast which would have to be celebrated on the sea.

"Had we but fire —" Torbek thrust his hands inside his cloak, trying to warm them a little. The ship rolled till she was almost on her beam ends; Torbek braced himself with practiced feet, but Cappen went into the bilge again.

He sprawled there for a while, his bruised body refusing movement. A weary sailor with a bucket glared at him through dripping hair. His shout was dim under the hoot and skirl of wind: "If ye like it so well down here, then help us bail!"

"'Tis not yet my turn," groaned Cappen, and got slowly up.

The wave which had nearly swamped them had put out the ship's fire and drenched the wood beyond hope of lighting a new one. It was cold fish and sea-sodden hardtack till they saw land again — if they ever did.

As Cappen raised himself on the leeward side, he thought he saw something gleam, far out across the wrathful night. A wavering red spark — He brushed a stiffened hand across his eyes, wondering if the madness of wind and water had struck through into his own skull. A gust of sleet hid it again. But —

He fumbled his way aft between the benches. Huddled figures cursed him wearily as he stepped on them. The ship shook herself, rolled along the edge of a boiling black trough, and slid down into it; for an instant, the white teeth of combers grinned above her rail, and Cappen waited for an end to all things. Then she mounted them again, somehow, and wallowed toward another valley.

King Svearek had the steering oar and was trying to hold the longboat into the wind. He had stood there since sundown, huge and untiring, legs braced and the bucking wood cradled in his arms. More than human he seemed, there under the icicle loom of the sternpost, his grey hair and beard rigid with ice. Beneath the horned helmet, the strong moody face turned right and left, peering into the darkness. Cappen felt smaller than usual when he approached the steersman.

He leaned close to the king, shouting against the blast of winter: "My lord, did I not see firelight?"

"Aye. I spied it an hour ago," grunted the king. "Been trying to steer us a little closer to it."

Cappen nodded, too sick and weary to feel reproved. "What is it?"

"Some island — there are many in this stretch of water — now shut up!"

Cappen crouched down under the rail and waited.

The lonely red gleam seemed nearer when he looked again. Svearek's tones were lifting in a roar that hammered through the gale from end to end of the ship: "Hither! Come hither to me, all men not working!"

Slowly, they groped to him, great shadowy forms in wool and leather, bulking over Cappen like storm-gods. Svearek nodded toward the flickering glow. "One of the islands, somebody must be living there. I cannot bring the ship closer for fear of surf, but one of ye should be able to take the boat thither and fetch us fire and dry wood. Who will go?"

They peered overside, and the uneasy movement that ran among them came from more than the roll and pitch of the deck underfoot.

Beorna the Bold spoke at last, it was hardly to be heard in the noisy dark: "I never knew of men living hereabouts. It must be a lair of trolls."

"Aye, so . . . aye, they'd but eat the man we sent . . . out oars, let's away from here though it cost our lives . . ." The frightened mumble was low under the jeering wind.

Svearek's face drew into a snarl. "Are ye men or puling babes? Hack yer way through them, if they be trolls, but bring me fire!"

"Even a she-troll is stronger than fifty men, my king," cried Torbek. "Well ye know that, when the monster woman broke through our guards three years ago and bore off Hildigund."

"Enough!" It was a scream in Svearek's throat. "I'll have yer craven heads for this, all of ye, if ye gang not to the isle!"

They looked at each other, the big men of Norren, and their shoulders hunched bearlike. It was Beorna who spoke it for them: "No, that ye will not. We are free housecarls, who will fight for a leader — but not for a madman."

Cappen drew back against the rail, trying to make himself small.

"All gods turn their faces from ye!" It was more than weariness and despair which glared in Svearek's eyes, there was something of death in them. "I'll go myself, then!"

"No, my king. That we will not find ourselves in."

"I am the king!"

"And we are yer housecarls, sworn to defend ye — even from yerself. Ye shall not go."

The ship rolled again, so violently that they were all thrown to starboard. Cappen landed on Torbek, who reached up to shove him aside and then closed one huge fist on his tunic.

"Here's our man!"

"Hi!" yelled Cappen.

Torbek hauled him roughly back to his feet. "Ye cannot row or bail yer fair share," he growled, "nor do ye know the rigging or any skill of a sailor — 'tis time ye made yerself useful!"

"Aye, aye — let little Cappen go — mayhap he can sing the trolls to sleep —" The laughter was hard and barking, edged with fear, and they all hemmed him in.

"My lord!" bleated the minstrel. "I am your guest —"

Svearek laughed unpleasantly, half crazily. "Sing them a song," he howled. "Make a fine roun — whatever ye call it — to the troll-wife's beauty. And bring us some fire, little man, bring us a flame less hot than the love in yer breast for yer lady!"

Teeth grinned through matted beards. Someone hauled on the rope from which the ship's small boat trailed, dragging it close. "Go, ye scut!" A horny hand sent Cappen stumbling to the rail.

He cried out once again. An ax lifted above his head. Someone handed him his own slim sword, and for a wild moment he thought of fighting. Useless — too many of them. He buckled on the sword and spat at the men. The wind tossed it back in his face, and they raved with laughter.

Over the side! The boat rose to meet him, he landed in a heap on drenched planks and looked up into the shadowy faces of the northmen. There was a sob in his throat as he found the seat and took out the oars.

An awkward pull sent him spinning from the ship, and then the night had swallowed it and he was alone. Numbly, he bent to the task. Unless he wanted to drown, there was no place to go but the island.

He was too weary and ill to be much afraid, and such fear as he had was all of the sea. It could rise over him, gulp him down, the grey horses would gallop over him and the long weeds would wrap him when he rolled dead against some skerry. The soft vales of Caronne and the roses in Croy's gardens seemed like a dream. There was only the roar and boom of the northern sea, hiss of sleet and spindrift, crazed scream of wind, he was alone as man had ever been and he would go down to the sharks alone.

The boat wallowed, but rode the waves better than the longship. He grew dully aware that the storm was pushing him toward the island. It was becoming visible, a deeper blackness harsh against the night.

He could not row much in the restless water, he shipped the oars and waited for the gale to capsize him and fill his mouth with the sea. And when it gurgled in his throat, what would his last thought be? Should he dwell on the lovely image of Ydris in Seilles, she of the long bright hair and the singing voice? But then there had been the tomboy laughter of dark Falkny, he could not neglect her. And there were memories of Elvanna in her castle by the lake, and Sirann of the Hundred Rings, and beauteous Vardry, and hawk-proud Lona, and — No, he could not do justice to any

of them in the little time that remained. What a pity
it was!

No, wait, that unforgettable night in Nienne, the
beauty which had whispered in his ear and drawn him
close, the hair which had fallen like a silken tent about
his cheeks . . . ah, that had been the summit of his life,
he would go down into darkness with her name on his
lips . . . But hell! What *had* her name been, now?

Cappen Varra, minstrel of Croy, clung to the bench
and sighed.

The great hollow voice of surf lifted about him,
waves sheeted across the gunwale and the boat danced
in madness. Cappen groaned, huddling into the circle
of his own arms and shaking with cold. Swiftly, now,
the end of all sunlight and laughter, the dark and
lonely road which all men must tread. *O Ilwarra of Syr,
Aedra in Tholis, could I but kiss you once more —*

Stones grated under the keel. It was a shock like a
sword going through him. Cappen looked unbeliev-
ingly up. The boat had drifted to land — he was alive!

It was like the sun in his breast. Weariness fell from
him, and he leaped overside, not feeling the chill of
the shallows. With a grunt, he heaved the boat up on
the narrow strand and knotted the painter to a fanglike
jut of reef.

Then he looked about him. The island was small,
utterly bare, a savage loom of rock rising out of the sea
that growled at its feet and streamed off its shoulders.
He had come into a little cliff-walled bay, somewhat
sheltered from the wind. He was here!

For a moment he stood, running through all he had
learned about the trolls which infested these north-
lands. Hideous and soulless dwellers underground,
they knew not old age; a sword could hew them asun-
der, but before it reached their deep-seated life, their

unhuman strength had plucked a man apart. Then they ate him —

Small wonder the northmen feared them. Cappen threw back his head and laughed. He had once done a service for a mighty wizard in the south, and his reward hung about his neck, a small silver amulet. The wizard had told him that no supernatural being could harm anyone who carried a piece of silver.

The northmen said that a troll was powerless against a man who was not afraid; but, of course, only to see one was to feel the heart turn to ice. They did not know the value of silver, it seemed — odd that they shouldn't, but they did not. Because Cappen Varra did, he had no reason to be afraid; therefore he was doubly safe, and it was but a matter of talking the troll into giving him some fire. If indeed there was a troll here, and not some harmless fisherman.

He whistled gaily, wrung some of the water from his cloak and ruddy hair, and started along the beach. In the sleety gloom, he could just see a hewn-out path winding up one of the cliffs and he set his feet on it.

At the top of the path, the wind ripped his whistling from his lips. He hunched his back against it and walked faster, swearing as he stumbled on hidden rocks. The ice-sheathed ground was slippery underfoot, and the cold bit like a knife.

Rounding a crag, he saw redness glow in the face of a steep bluff. A cave mouth, a fire within — he hastened his steps, hungering for warmth, until he stood in the entrance.

"Who comes?"

It was a hoarse bass cry that rang and boomed between walls of rock; there was ice and horror in it, for a moment Cappen's heart stumbled. Then he remembered the amulet and strode boldly inside.

"Good evening, mother," he said cheerily.

The cave widened out into a stony hugeness that gaped with tunnels leading further underground. The rough, soot-blackened walls were hung with plundered silks and cloth-of-gold, gone ragged with age and damp; the floor was strewn with stinking rushes, and gnawed bones were heaped in disorder. Cappen saw the skulls of men among them. In the center of the room, a great fire leaped and blazed, throwing billows of heat against him; some of its smoke went up a hole in the roof, the rest stung his eyes to watering and he sneezed.

The troll-wife crouched on the floor, snarling at him. She was quite the most hideous thing Cappen had ever seen: nearly as tall as he, she was twice as broad and thick, and the knotted arms hung down past bowed knees till their clawed fingers brushed the ground. Her head was beastlike, almost split in half by the tusked mouth, the eyes wells of darkness, the nose an ell long; her hairless skin was green and cold, moving on her bones. A tattered shift covered some of her monstrousness, but she was still a nightmare.

"Ho-ho, ho-ho!" Her laughter roared out, hungry and hollow as the surf around the island. Slowly, she shuffled closer. "So my dinner comes walking in to greet me, ho, ho, ho! Welcome, sweet flesh, welcome, good marrow-filled bones, come in and be warmed."

"Why, thank you, good mother." Cappen shucked his cloak and grinning at her through the smoke. He felt his clothes steaming already. "I love you too."

Over her shoulder, he suddenly saw the girl. She was huddled in a corner, wrapped in fear, but the eyes that watched him were as blue as the skies over Caronne. The ragged dress did not hide the gentle curves of her body, nor did the tear-streaked grime spoil the lilt of her face. "Why, 'tis springtime in here," cried Cappen, "and Primavera herself is strewing flowers of love."

"What are you talking about, crazy man?" rumbled the troll-wife. She turned to the girl. "Heap the fire, Hildigund, and set up the roasting spit. Tonight I feast!"

"Truly I see heaven in female form before me," said Cappen.

The troll scratched her misshapen head.

"You must surely be from far away, moonstruck man," she said.

"Aye, from golden Croy am I wandered, drawn over dolorous seas and empty wild lands by the fame of loveliness waiting here; and now that I have seen you, my life is full." Cappen was looking at the girl as he spoke, but he hoped the troll might take it as aimed her way.

"It will be fuller," grinned the monster. "Stuffed with hot coals while yet you live." She glanced back at the girl. "What, are you not working yet, you lazy tub of lard? Set up the spit, I said!"

The girl shuddered back against a heap of wood. "No," she whispered. "I cannot — not . . . not for a man."

"Can and will, my girl," said the troll, picking up a bone to throw at her. The girl shrieked a little.

"No, no, sweet mother. I would not be so ungallant as to have beauty toil for me." Cappen plucked at the troll's filthy dress. "It is not meet — in two senses. I only came to beg a little fire; yet will I bear away a greater fire within my heart."

"Fire in your guts, you mean! No man ever left me save as picked bones."

Cappen thought he heard a worried note in the animal growl. "Shall we have music for the feast?" he asked mildly. He unslung the case of his harp and took it out.

The troll-wife waved her fists in the air and danced with rage. "Are you mad? I tell you, you are going to be eaten!"

The minstrel plucked a string on his harp. "This wet air has played the devil with her tone," he murmured sadly.

The troll-wife roared wordlessly and lunged at him. Hildigund covered her eyes. Cappen tuned his harp. A foot from his throat, the claws stopped.

"Pray do not excite yourself, mother," said the bard. "I carry silver, you know."

"What is that to me? If you think you have a charm which will turn me, know that there is none. I've no fear of your metal!"

Cappen threw back his head and sang:

"A lovely lady full oft lies.
The light that lies within her eyes
And lies and lies, in no surprise.
All her unkindness can devise
To trouble hearts that seek the prize
Which is herself, are angel lies —"

"*Aaaarrrgh!*" It was like thunder drowning him out. The troll-wife turned and went on all fours and poked up the fire with her nose.

Cappen stepped softly around her and touched the girl. She looked up with a little whimper.

"You are Svearek's only daughter, are you not?" he whispered.

"Aye —" She bowed her head, a strengthless despair weighting it down. "The troll stole me away three winters agone. It has tickled her to have a princess for slave — but soon I will roast on her spit, even as ye, brave man —"

"Ridiculous. So fair a lady is meant for another kind of, um, never mind! Has she treated you very ill?"

"She beats me now and again — and I have been so lonely, naught here at all save the troll-wife and I —" The small work-roughened hands clutched desperately at his waist, and she buried her face against his breast.

"Can ye save us?" she gasped. "I fear 'tis for naught ye ventured yer life, bravest of men. I fear we'll soon both sputter on the coals."

Cappen said nothing. If she wanted to think he had come especially to rescue her, he would not be so ungallant to tell her otherwise.

The troll-wife's mouth gashed in a grin as she walked through the fire to him. "There is a price," she said. "If you cannot tell me three things about myself which are true beyond disproving, not courage nor amulet nor the gods themselves may avail to keep that red head on your shoulders."

Cappen clapped a hand to his sword. "Why, gladly," he said; this was a rule of magic he had learned long ago, that three truths were the needful armor to make any guardian charm work. "Imprimis, yours is the ugliest nose I ever saw poking up a fire. Secundus, I was never in a house I cared less to guest at. Tertius, ever among trolls you are little liked, being one of the worst."

Hildigund moaned with terror as the monster swelled in rage. But there was no movement. Only the leaping flames and the eddying smoke stirred.

Cappen's voice rang out, coldly: "Now the king lies on the sea, frozen and wet, and I am come to fetch a brand for his fire. And I had best also see his daughter home."

The troll shook her head, suddenly chuckling. "No. The brand you may have, just to get you out of this cave, foulness; but the woman is in my thrall until a man sleeps with her — here — for a night. And if he does, I may have him to break my fast in the morning!"

Cappen yawned mightily. "Thank you, mother. Your offer of a bed is most welcome to these tired bones, and I accept gratefully."

"You will die tomorrow!" she raved. The ground shook under the huge weight of her as she stamped. "Because of the three truths, I must let you go tonight; but tomorrow I may do what I will!"

"Forget not my little friend, mother," said Cappen, and touched the cord of the amulet.

"I tell you, silver has no use against me —"

Cappen sprawled on the floor and rippled fingers across his harp. *"A lovely lady full oft lies —"*

The troll-wife turned from him in a rage. Hildigund ladled up some broth, saying nothing, and Cappen ate it with pleasure, though it could have used more seasoning.

After that he indited a sonnet to the princess, who regarded him wide-eyed. The troll came back from a tunnel after he finished, and said curtly: "This way." Cappen took the girl's hand and followed her into a pitchy, reeking dark.

She plucked an arras aside to show a room which surprised him by being hung with tapestries, lit with candles, and furnished with a fine broad featherbed. "Sleep here tonight, if you dare," she growled. "And tomorrow I shall eat you — and you, worthless lazy she-trash, will have the hide flayed off your back!" She barked a laugh and left them.

Hildigund fell weeping on the mattress. Cappen let her cry herself out while he undressed and got between the blankets. Drawing his sword, he laid it carefully in the middle of the bed.

The girl looked at him through jumbled fair locks. "How can ye dare?" she whispered. "One breath of fear, one moment's doubt, and the troll is free to rend ye."

"Exactly." Cappen yawned. "Doubtless she hopes that fear will come to me lying wakeful in the night. Wherefore 'tis but a question of going gently to sleep. O Svearek, Torbek, and Beorna, could you but see how I am resting now!"

"But . . . the three truths ye gave her . . . how knew ye. . .?"

"Oh, those. Well, see you, sweet lady, Primus and Secundus were my own thoughts, and who is to disprove them? Tertius was also clear, since you said there had been no company here in three years — yet are there many trolls in these lands, ergo even they cannot stomach our gentle hostess." Cappen watched her through heavy-lidded eyes.

She flushed deeply, blew out the candles, and he heard her slip off her garment and get in with him. There was a long silence.

Then: "Are ye not —"

"Yes, fair one?" he muttered through his drowsiness.

"Are ye not . . . well, I am here and ye are here and —"

"Fear not," he said. "I laid my sword between us. Sleep in peace."

"I . . . would be glad — ye have come to deliver —"

"No, fair lady. No man of gentle breeding could so abuse his power. Goodnight." He leaned over, brushing his lips gently across hers, and lay down again.

"Ye are . . . I never thought man could be so noble," she whispered.

Cappen mumbled something. As his soul spun into sleep, he chuckled. Those unresting days and nights on the sea had not left him fit for that kind of exercise. But, of course, if she wanted to think he was being magnanimous, it could be useful later —

*H*e woke with a start and looked into the sputtering glare of a torch. Its light wove across the crags and gullies of the troll-wife's face and shimmered wetly off the great tusks in her mouth.

"Good morning, mother," said Cappen politely.

Hildigund thrust back a scream.

"Come and be eaten," said the troll-wife.

"No, thank you," said Cappen, regretfully but firmly. "'Twould be ill for my health. No, I will but trouble you for a firebrand and then the princess and I will be off."

"If you think that stupid bit of silver will protect you, think again," she snapped. "Your three sentences were all that saved you last night. Now I hunger."

"Silver," said Cappen didactically, "is a certain shield against all black magics. So the wizard told me, and he was such a nice white-bearded old man I am sure even his attendant devils never lied. Now please depart, mother, for modesty forbids me to dress before your eyes."

The hideous face thrust close to his. He smiled dreamily and tweaked her nose — hard.

She howled and flung the torch at him. Cappen caught it and stuffed it into her mouth. She choked and ran from the room.

"A new sport — trollbaiting," said the bard gaily into the sudden darkness. "Come, shall we not venture out?"

The girl trembled too much to move. He comforted her, absentmindedly, and dressed in the dark, swearing at the clumsy leggings. When he left, Hildigund put on her clothes and hurried after him.

The troll-wife squatted by the fire and glared at them as they went by. Cappen hefted his sword and looked at her. "I do not love you," he said mildly, and hewed out.

She backed away, shrieking as he slashed at her. In the end, she crouched at the mouth of a tunnel, raging futilely. Cappen pricked her with his blade.

"It is not worth my time to follow you down underground," he said, "but if ever you trouble men again, I will hear of it and come and feed you to my dogs. A piece at a time — a very small piece — do you understand?"

She snarled at him.

"An *extremely* small piece," said Cappen amiably. "Have you heard me?"

Something broke in her. "Yes," she whimpered. He let her go, and she scuttled from him like a rat.

He remembered the firewood and took an armful; on the way, he thoughtfully picked up a few jeweled rings which he didn't think she would be needing and stuck them in his pouch. Then he led the girl outside.

The wind had laid itself, a clear frosty morning glittered on the sea and the longship was a distant sliver against white-capped blueness. The minstrel groaned. "What a distance to row! Oh, well —"

*T*hey were at sea before Hildigund spoke. Awe was in the eyes that watched him. "No man could be so brave," she murmured. "Are ye a god?"

"Not quite," said Cappen. "No, most beautiful one, modesty grips my tongue. 'Twas but that I had the silver and was therefore proof against her sorcery."

"But the silver was no help!" she cried.

Cappen's oar caught a crab. "What?" he yelled.

"No — no — why, she told ye so her own self —"

"I thought she lied. I *know* the silver guards against —"

"But she used no magic! Trolls have but their own strength!"

Cappen sagged in his seat. For a moment he thought he was going to faint. Then only his lack of fear had armored him; and if he had known the truth, that would not have lasted a minute.

He laughed shakily. Another score for his doubts about the overall value of truth!

The longship's oars bit water and approached him. Indignant voices asking why he had been so long on his errand faded when his passenger was seen. And Svearek the king wept as he took his daughter back into his arms.

The hard brown face was still blurred with tears when he looked at the minstrel, but the return of his old self was there too. "What ye have done, Cappen Varra of Croy, is what no other man in the world could have done."

"Aye — aye —" The rough northern voices held adoration as the warriors crowded around the slim red-haired figure.

"Ye shall have her whom ye saved to wife," said Svearek, "and when I die ye shall rule all Norren."

Cappen swayed and clutched the rail.

Three nights later he slipped away from their shore camp and turned his face southward.